Sr. Marguerite

Sr. Marguerite

BILLY
and his friends
discover their mission.

Text by Kevin Donovan
Illustration by Tom Donovan

Library of Congress Catalog Number: TXu 601-516
Donovan, Kevin M.
"Billy And His Friends Discover Their Mission"
Printed by Reynolds Printing, Inc., Eden Prairie, MN

Not long ago a group of little bears were sleeping in their beds in an orphanage.

Billy Bear was sound asleep with a smile on his face. He was dreaming that a heavenly bear with wings was talking to him.

Billy Bear suddenly sat up and wanted to know, "Who is that talking to me?" To Billy's surprise, a bear with wings

was hovering over him, talking to Billy and on his paw sat a
little white dove with a halo.

The bear with wings left soon after, but the little white dove remained and sat on Billy's paw. By this time, all of the other bears had joined Billy on his bed to see what was happening. Then, the little white dove spoke to them.

"Your mission in life is to leave the orphanage and go into the forest to find a church which has the San Damiano Cross hanging at the altar."

Without another word, the dove flew up towards heaven.

Using his flashlight,
Billy and his friends spent
several hours in the library
searching through hundreds
of books. Suddenly Billy
shouted, "Here it is. This
is the Cross the little white
dove told us to find."

"Who is St. Francis, Billy? Why did God talk to him?",
questioned the other bears.

San Damiano Cross.

This Cross talked to St. Francis.
It was Jesus telling Francis to go
and help change the Church.

"Don't know, but we must leave and look for the little church
in the forest and find out," Billy answered.

So Billy and the bears prayed.

"Oh God, please help us find the church in the forest that the little white dove told us about. The Church has the San Damiano Cross hanging at the altar."

"Follow me, and we will go into the forest and ask all of the animals where the little church is."

Billy and his friends journeyed into the forest and before long met Tucan, the bird. "Hi, my name is Billy. All of us bears are trying to find the little church in the forest. Can you point out which way we go?"

"Yes I can," Tucan replied.
"This is the path you take.
 You will run into some tall trees. Look for a sign on
 one of the trees that says 'San Damiano Church'."

The bears continued down the path and soon they saw a church in the distance with someone standing in the doorway.

"Look Billy, the sign says, 'San Damiano Church'," they exclaimed.

Billy approaches the church. "Hello, my name is Billy Bear and these are my friends. We came to find the church that the little white dove with the halo has told us about.

It has the San Damiano Cross hanging at the altar. We want to find out who St. Francis is and about the little white dove with the halo."

"Hi Billy, my name is Pastor Bob, and you have found the Church of San Damiano. Let's go into the church and I will show you the cross."

Pastor Bob explains,

"This is the San Damiano Cross that talked to St. Francis. It was Jesus's voice telling Francis to help change the church. Francis was a saint who loved all the animals. The little white dove who talked to you, Billy, is the Holy Spirit, the third person of the Holy Trinity. He gives us love to help all the animals in the forest, just like Francis did."

"The Holy Spirit must love you a lot Billy."

Outside the bears gathered around a camp fire to learn more. Pastor Bob said, "I wanted to talk to you bears about how great it is that you are following Francis in his love for all creatures in the forest. He was a special person who talked to the birds and all the small animals. They loved

him so much that they stopped all their singing just to listen to him. So, your mission in life is to be like Francis and help all living things and to love each other as Francis did."

The bears felt good knowing they, too, were special and had a mission in life.

"It is time to start your journey. Goodbye Billy, and all of you brother bears," said Pastor Bob. As Billy and the other bears were leaving Pastor Bob remembered the words of St. Francis and said,

"Be praised, my Lord, for Brother Sun and Sister Moon.
Be praised, my Lord, for Brother Wind and Sister Winter.
Be praised, my Lord, for Mother Earth. Praise and bless
the Lord who will follow you on your journey."